I Live in Tokyo

Department store workers welcome the first shoppers of the day.

For my mother, who lives in Tokyo

Calligraphy by Naoko Tomioka

All rights reserved. For information about permission to reproduce
selections from this book, write to Permissions, Houghton Mifflin Company,
215 Park Avenue South, New York, New York 10003.

www.houghtonmifflinbooks.com

The text of this book is set in 14-point Hiroshige Medium.
The illustrations are watercolor.

Library of Congress Cataloging-in-Publication Data

Takabayashi, Mari.
I live in Tokyo / written and illustrated by Mari Takabayashi.
p. cm.
1. Tokyo (Japan)—Social life and customs—Juvenile literature.
2. Tokyo (Japan)—Anniversaries, etc.—Juvenile literature. [1. Tokyo (Japan)—
Social life and customs. 2. Japan—Social life and customs.]
DS896.5 .I3 2001   952'.135—dc21   00-05964

Manufactured in Singapore
TWP 10 9 8 7 6 5 4 3 2

We hang the *futon* outside on sunny days.

Many women go shopping by bicycle.

I Live in Tokyo

written & illustrated by

Mari Takabayashi

Houghton Mifflin Company Boston

The *futon* closet, called *oshiire,* is a good
hideout when we play hide-and-seek.

We chat with visitors in the *genkan,*
the entrance hall.

I live in the city of *Tokyo,* in Japan.

The area of the city with many restaurants and shops is called *Ginza.*

The super gigantic buildings around *Shinjuku,* Tokyo

Akihabara is the electronics shopping district.

The Royal Palace

Japan is an Asian country on a group of islands in the Pacific Ocean.
Tokyo is the capital. My grandparents live in *Kobe*.

My name is Mimiko. I am seven years old. Kenta, my little brother, is five.
We live with our parents in downtown *Tokyo,* in a small house on a street
with many neighbors.

nengajo
New Year's greeting cards

osechi ryori
sweet and salty side dishes

ozoni
soup made with sweet rice cakes and vegetables

otoshidama
New Year's gift money given to children

Akemashite omedeto gozaimasu! Happy New Year! I love *oshogatsu*, the New Year celebration. I can eat all the tasty food I want and my parents don't ask me if I did my homework. After brunch, we go to the *Shinto* shrine for the first visit of the year.

kagami mochi
**specially decorated
rice cakes**

hagoita
**wooden racket for
Japanese badminton**

eto
**Japanese zodiac,
based on
twelve animals**

My mother is a master of *shodo,* or calligraphy. It is said that January 2 is perfect for writing, so we spread newspaper all over the *tatami* room to protect the mats from the ink. I write *"yume,"* which means "dream." *Shodo* makes me feel calm.

The day before the first day of spring, February 3, is called *setsubun*. We pretend to drive out misfortune by throwing handfuls of dried soybeans to the demon called *Oni*. My father puts on the *Oni* mask, and Kenta and I shout, "Out with the ogre! In with the happiness!" My father is a very funny *Oni*.

On Valentine's Day, girls give chocolates to boys. I buy many chocolates and give them to my teacher, my father, and the boys I know. This year my father gets more chocolates than my brother. He looks really happy!

On March 3 we have a festival called *Hinamatsuri*, the Doll's Festival, to pray for young girls' growth and happiness. My grandparents gave me a *hina ningyo* set when I was born, and each year my mother decorates the dolls a few weeks before the day.

chirashi zushi
rice with vegetables or fish

suimono
clam soup

amazake
a special drink
for children

hina arare
sweet rice crackers

This year we visit my grandparents' house for dinner. We eat *chirashi zushi* and clam soup, as we do every year. My grandmother's homemade *sushi* is the best. It's a special night.

my textbooks

notebooks

paper for essays

bento box

school lunch

bag for gym uniform

randoseru
red leather knapsack for books

I start second grade this April. My new teacher, Yamada-*sensei,* is kind. Kenta, a kindergartner, is in school for the first time. I wear a special hat, and Kenta wears a cute uniform. Kenta brings a *bento* box for lunch, but I eat in the cafeteria.

mother

bird

tree

Kenta

Mimiko

mountain

river

fire

mouth

sun

fish

eye

In class we study Japanese writing. *Kanji* are Chinese characters, based on pictures, that are used in Japanese writing. There are hundreds of characters to learn, and the teacher tests us every day. Sometimes it's tough. The *kanji* in Kenta's name mean "healthy and big." The *kanji* in Mimiko mean "beautiful."

五月

MAY GOGATSU

May 5 is *Tango no Sekku,* Boys' Festival, a day honoring little boys.
We fly carp streamers in our garden and display *samurai* warrior dolls
in our living room.

My Top Ten Favorite Meals

1. curry rice

2. *tempura*
deep-fried vegetables
and shrimp

Japanese-style apron

3. omelet rice

4. hamburger

5. *yakitori*
grilled chicken on skewers

6. *yakizakana*
grilled fish

7. *oden*
fish cake stew

8. *nimono*
simmered vegetables

9. *katsudon*
pork cutlet bowl

10. *sukiyaki*
beef and vegetable dish

My grandmother is a master of *sado,* the tea ceremony. She has a tea ceremony room in her house next to a beautiful Japanese garden. My family is invited to the tea ceremony several times a year.

My grandmother says this is a precious time for her because she can relax. But the long ceremony gets boring and my feet fall asleep. We try not to gobble the fancy and delicious *wagashi* cakes.

The temple in our neighborhood has a special fair, or *Ennichi,* in July. Vendors come to the temple with cotton candy, fried noodles, barbecued corn, balloons, and masks. We fish for goldfish and win prizes. So much fun!

At the *Bon* Festival, there is an area where everyone dances—old and young, men and women. Even Kenta and I start dancing when we hear the *bon odori* dance music.

In August we visit my grandparents in the country. We take the *shinkansen,* the bullet train, one of the fastest trains in the world.

I play for hours with our cousins—fishing, climbing trees, finding bugs. One night we have fireworks, and even my grandfather comes outside to watch.

A special day is my cousin Michiko's wedding, which was planned for a lucky day on the Japanese calendar. She wears a traditional *kimono*, then changes into a wedding dress. She is so beautiful.

Every day after school, I walk home with my friend Yoko-*chan* because we are neighbors. She often comes to my house with me. We play with dolls, do *origami,* or watch TV.

On a nice day in October, my school has a field day, called *undokai*.
The classes split up into teams and compete against each other.

This year our class is on the red team. I am in the obstacle race and I come in second! I also join the tug of war.

November 15 is *Shichigosan*. Boys who are three and five years old and girls who are three and seven put on *kimonos* and go to the shrine to pray for children's growth. The *kimono* makes me feel like a princess, but after a while it's uncomfortable. I can't run, and the *obi* around my belly starts to itch.

How to wear a *kimono*

Toji is the first day of winter, around December 22. We take a bath with *yuzu* oranges. The yuzu bath makes our bodies warm and smooth.

Every year my mother bakes a Christmas cake and we decorate a Christmas tree. Even though we don't celebrate this holiday, it is still a fun tradition.

On New Year's Eve, the hair salons are crowded with women who will wear a *kimono* the next day.

Omisoka, New Year's Eve, is cleanup day. Then my mother lets us stay up to watch TV while she cooks special noodles at midnight. After we hear *joya no kane,* the New Year's Eve bells, we go to bed. It has been a wonderful year!

Months of the year

Ichigatsu (ee-chee-gah-tsu): January

Nigatsu (nee-gah-tsu): February

Sangatsu (sahn-gah-tsu): March

Shigatsu (shee-gah-tsu): April

Gogatsu (goh-gah-tsu): May

Rokugatsu (roh-koo-gah-tsu): June

Shichigatsu (shee-chee-gah-tsu): July

Hachigatsu (hah-chee-gah-tsu): August

Kugatsu (koo-gah-tsu): September

Jugatsu (joo-gah-tsu): October

Juichigatsu (joo-ee-chee-gah-tsu): November

Junigatsu (joo-nee-gah-tsu): December

A few words

bon odori (bon oh-doh-ree): dance performed at the *Bon* Festival, a Buddhist event honoring ancestors

-chan (chan): name suffix showing close friendship

futon (foo-tahn): foldable mattress

hina ningyo (hee-nah neen-gyoh): traditional dolls that represent the emperor and empress from the Heian period (794–1192)

origami (oh-ree-gah-mee): Japanese art of folding paper to create animals, flowers, or other pretty shapes

samurai (sa-moo-rah-ee): ancient Japanese warrior

sensei (sen-say): word or suffix meaning teacher

Shinto shrine (shin-toh): temple where Shinto deities honoring nature and ancestors are enshrined

sushi (soo-shee): combinations of rice and raw fish, often fashioned in small pieces to be picked up and eaten with the fingers

tatami (tah-tah-mee): Japanese straw floor mat

Numbers

ichi one	*go* five	*ku* nine
ni two	*roku* six	*ju* ten
san three	*shichi* seven	*juichi* eleven
shi four	*hachi* eight	*juni* twelve

Speaking in Japanese

Konnichiwa.
(kohn-nee-chee-wah)
Good afternoon.

Watashi no namae wa Mimiko desu.
(wah-tah-shee noh nah-mah-eh wah Mee-mee-koh des)
My name is Mimiko.

Watashi wa nanasai desu.
(wah-tah-shee wah nah-nah-sah-ee des)
I am seven years old.

Watashi wa Tokyo ni sunde imasu.
(wah-tah-shee wah toh-kyoh nee sun-deh ee-mas)
I live in Tokyo.

Doomo arigato.
(doh-moh ah-ree-gah-toh)
Thank you.

Doo itashimashite.
(doh ee-tah-shee-mah-shee-tay)
You are welcome.

Sumimasen.
(soo-mee-mah-sen)
Excuse me.

Akemashite omedeto gozaimasu.
(ah-kay-mah-shee-tay oh-may-day-toh goh-zah-ee-mas)
Happy New Year!

Irasshai mase.
(ee-rah-shah-ee mah-say)
Come in! Welcome!

Sayonara.
(sah-yoh-nah-rah)
Goodbye.